Adapted by M. C. King

Based on the television series *Hannah Montana*, created by Michael Poryes and Rich Correll and Barry O'Brien

Part One is based on the episode written by Lisa Albert

Part Two is based on the episode written by Howard Meyers

First published by Parragon in 2007
Parragon
Queen Street House
4 Queen Street
Bath BA1 1HE, UK

ISBN 978-1-4075-0242-7
Printed in United kingdom

PART ONE

Chapter One

As Miley Stewart stared at the screen of her laptop computer, she could practically hear her best friend Lilly's heart beating. Lilly was Miley's confidante and constant companion, and right now she was reading over Miley's shoulder.

"This is so cool!" Lilly yelped. "I can't believe how many people email Hannah Montana."

From the looks of it, Miley appeared to be your average eighth grader. But Miley, mild-mannered junior high school student by day, had a secret. She was also Hannah Montana, pop superstar. Only a few people knew Miley was the normal girl behind mega-successful Hannah's awesome disguises. Lilly was one of them.

Miley read off the computer screen: "'Dear Hannah, you rock. Jill in Milwaukee'."

So sweet!

"'Dear Hannah, you're awesome! Danny in Iowa City'."

Cool.

"'Dear Hannah, get your bra off the shower rod. Jackson in Malibu'."

Ewww.

And, huh? Jackson in Malibu? That was weird. Miley lived in Malibu, she had a brother named Jackson, and . . .

Duh.

Miley's brother, Jackson, still dripping wet from the shower, sloshed into the living room. He was dangling Miley's bra from his right index finger.

"And I mean it!" he grumbled, dropping the bra next to Miley.

Miley scowled. "He touched it," she complained, turning up her nose in disgust. "Now I have to burn it."

With the help of a letter opener, Miley lifted the bra and deposited it in the bin.

Lilly continued reading Hannah's fan letters. "'Dear Hannah, I love, love, love that scarf you wore at the video awards. Where, where, where can I get one? Jenny in Walla Walla, Washington'."

Miley scoured her brain to try to remember which scarf she'd worn to the video awards . . . Oh, yeah, the awesome orange one. She couldn't say she minded all the free clothes she got being Hannah Montana.

Miley opened the next email.

"Listen to this one," she told Lilly. "'Dear Hannah, I have this massive crush on a boy who doesn't know I exist'."

This letter was a little juicier than the rest.

"Typical," grumped Lilly, who'd had her share of unrequited crushes.

Miley kept reading: "'His locker is three down from mine. What should I do? Your biggest fan, Becca from Malibu'."

Malibu? Miley wondered if this was one of Jackson's stupid pranks. No, wait, Becca from Malibu, that sounded familiar . . .

Apparently, Lilly thought so too.

"You don't think it could be Becca Weller from homeroom?" she gasped.

Hmmmm, thought Miley. Is Becca my

biggest fan? She does wear Hannah Montana T-shirts a lot. But so do lots of people . . . but then Miley's mind wandered to Becca's locker, which, if she recalled correctly, was plastered with Hannah Montana paraphernalia: stickers, posters, photographs. Miley remembered how she'd been a little awed at Becca's collection, which included some rare one-of-a-kind . . .

According to Becca's letter, her crush's locker was three down from hers. In her head, Miley counted three down. There was Sandy Stringfellow, otherwise known as 'the Flosser', flossing her teeth. That didn't seem right. She counted three doors down the other way. No way, she thought. It couldn't be . . .

That locker belonged to Oliver Oken, one of Miley and Lilly's very best friends. Miley must have counted wrong. She

scanned her brain. One, two, three . . . She still landed on Oliver. She could just see him, standing before his messy locker, prying an old, half-licked lollipop from the inside shelf, then popping it into his mouth.

Apparently, Lilly's mind had gone to a similar place because together the girls emitted a cry of shock: "Oliver!"

"I can't believe it." Miley was astonished. "Becca Weller is crushing on Oliver."

While Lilly loved her friend Oliver, it was hard to imagine that anyone would have a crush on him. Was Becca Weller a total head case?

"Poor thing," she remarked, remembering back to fifth grade when they'd learned to do the uneven parallel bars. "She's never been quite right since that fall in gym class."

Meanwhile, Miley was mulling over what advice to give Becca. Oliver is way too dense to know when a girl likes him, she thought. He'd never make the first move. There was only one thing to do. She typed an email: "Dear Becca, if he won't ask you out, you ask him. Rock his world! Sincerely, Hannah Montana."

Miley reread her email, feeling pretty pleased with herself. She loved telling girls to take charge. It's what Hannah Montana would do, after all. "Making the world a better place for luuuuv . . ." Miley sang contentedly. She pressed SEND.

Just then, Jackson, dry now, entered the living room. He wore a dressing gown that was way too small.

"My robe fell in the toilet, so I borrowed yours. Hope you don't mind," he said, scratching his behind.

Miley's smile evaporated. "Now I gotta burn that, too!"

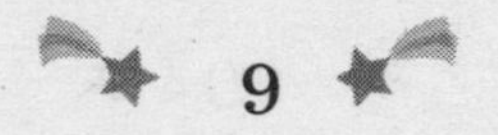

Chapter Two

The next morning at school, Miley and Lilly searched high and low for Becca Weller. Finally, they found her by the lockers. And three lockers down was Oliver! Miley counted again, just to be sure. Yup, no doubt about it. Becca was crushing on Oliver.

The girls observed Becca as if they were scientists and she was a rat they were experimenting on. They watched her move stuff from her rucksack into her locker: first a textbook, then three notebooks, then her PDA (probably the one she'd used to email Hannah Montana, Miley noted).

They paid attention to her every move: the way Becca tucked her hair behind her ear; how she patted her lower lip with her forefinger after putting on lip balm; how she turned towards Oliver and moved her eyes up and down, from the top of his head to the rubber bottoms of his trainers, as if to take everything in. *Classic once-over!* Miley thought. She elbowed Lilly.

"Did you see that?" she asked under her breath. "She totally checked him out."

"Definitely interested," Lilly replied with a nod.

They watched Becca spritz herself with perfume, then stroll past Oliver.

"Oooh!" Lilly squealed. She couldn't help being impressed by Becca's daring. "Perfume walk-by."

"First you see it, then you smell it!" Miley joked. "Kinda the opposite of my uncle Earl."

They kept watching as Becca made her way over to Oliver. When she tapped him on the shoulder, Miley could actually see Oliver's bony shoulder flinch.

"Uh . . . hi," Becca said. "Did you get the history assignment? I forgot to write it down."

Oliver had been talking to another boy. He actually looked annoyed to be interrupted.

"No, but Mr Aaron always writes it on the board," he answered plainly.

"Oh. Okay. I'll–" Before Becca could finish her sentence, Oliver had turned his back to her. "–go look. Thanks."

Miley couldn't help but cringe. She knew Oliver hadn't meant to spurn Becca, but that had been pretty harsh.

It wasn't like Miley to meddle. Really, it wasn't. The truth was, she was usually too busy to play Cupid to students at school. Being a major pop star was a huge time drain. But knowing how Becca felt, Miley couldn't just stand by and watch Oliver break her heart. This wasn't meddling, she told herself. This was a good deed. For a fan, no less. Maybe even her biggest fan . . .

So once poor, rejected Becca had left for class, Miley and Lilly made a beeline for Oliver.

"Oh, Oliver?" Miley said in a too-sweet sing-song voice. She turned to the boy he'd been talking to. "Excuse us," she said, sounding more businesslike.

Miley slapped the shoulder that Becca had gently tapped. This time Oliver more than flinched.

"What is wrong with you?" Miley asked him.

"Ow!" Oliver looked shocked as he rubbed his shoulder. "What'd I do?"

"Couldn't you see that Becca Weller was hitting on you?"

Oliver's mouth fell open. "What?"

Lilly slapped his other shoulder. "Geez! A grilled cheese sandwich would've picked up on that!"

Oliver was easily distracted – especially when food was concerned.

"They're serving grilled cheese today?" he asked excitedly.

This time, Miley and Lilly whacked Oliver's shoulders at once. Everyone knew guys were thick when it came to girls, but this was unbelievable! Miley tried to contain herself as she explained to Oliver that Becca was an A student who already knew what the history assignment was. Obviously, she didn't need to ask him for it.

"Then why'd she ask me?" Oliver cowered, preparing for the inevitable. "And don't hit me again!" he half warned, half begged.

This was beyond exasperating! What did Miley have to do, hit him? Wait, she'd already done that . . .

"Because she's crushin' on you," she told him in a tone that said 'Duh'.

"How do you know?" Oliver asked.

Aside from Lilly, Oliver was the only friend who knew about Miley's secret other life as Hannah Montana. Miley reminded him of that: "Remember how you had to spit-swear never to reveal my other identity?" she asked.

Oliver nodded. "Yes, and I got a cold right after that, thank you very much," he said with a grimace.

"Well, start sucking down some chicken soup," Miley told him. She paused, opened her hand, and spat on her palm. "Because another secret's coming your way."

Reluctantly, Oliver held his hand out. He turned his head as they shook. If he looked, he'd be too grossed out.

"I wish we hadn't outgrown the pinkie swear," he muttered under his breath.

Miley swivelled her head every which way to make sure the coast was clear, then whispered, "Becca emailed Hannah Montana. She said she had a big crush on you."

The news was finally dawning on Oliver.

"Becca Weller has a crush on me?" He pointed to himself to make sure *he* was the *you* Miley meant. "Me?"

"I know. We were shocked, too," Lilly admitted.

Oliver took several moments to contemplate the news, then broke into a smile. "So . . ." he suddenly sounded very psyched, "Becca Weller wants to take a ride on the Ollie Trolley." He motioned towards the cafeteria. "Let's go make her dreams come true." For extra effect he gestured with his hand as if pulling on an imaginary trolley bell. "Ding, ding!"

They watched Oliver strut off. Miley wondered if maybe she'd underestimated her friend. Here he was all gung ho about making the first move. But moments later, he came shuffling back.

"I forgot something," he said sheepishly.

"What?" Miley asked.

"My name! But I know it rhymes with trolley . . ."

He departed, defeated, to mull it over.

"That boy doesn't have the brains the good Lord gave a hunk o' turkey jerky," said Miley with a smile.

Chapter Three

That afternoon, a beleaguered Oliver joined Miley's brother, Jackson, and Jackson's friend Cooper at Rico's, a beach-front cafe. He needed a little male-bonding session to soothe his wounded ego.

"I don't get it, man. What happened to Oliver Smokin' Oken?" asked Cooper, sitting at the counter while Jackson, who worked at Rico's after school, sponged it down.

"I just totally froze." Just saying it out loud made Oliver's stomach sink into his trainers. "Has that ever happened to you?" he asked Jackson.

He was desperate to feel that he wasn't the only loser out there.

"Has that ever happened to him?" asked Cooper, barely suppressing a belly laugh.

Oh, so maybe he wasn't the only one, Oliver thought hopefully. But his hopes of getting a sympathetic sob story out of Jackson were quickly dashed.

"It's never happened to me," said Jackson matter-of-factly.

Just then, Robby Stewart, Jackson and Miley's dad, jogged up.

"Gimme a water, son," he panted. "I swear, there's nothing better than a ten-mile run on the beach. Someday I'll know what that feels like." He turned to Oliver.

"Hey, buddy, Miley told me about the Ollie Trolley's little derailment."

News sure travelled fast in Malibu!

"Oh, man, why don't we just put it in the newspaper?" Oliver said, annoyed.

"Look, it's nothin' to be embarrassed about," Mr Stewart said in that Dad-knows-best kind of way. "You know how I got my first date? I walked right up to her, looked her straight in the eye, and said, 'My Robby name is hi'."

At least he remembered his name, thought Oliver. Still, Mr Stewart's story gave him a smidgen of relief.

"And that worked?" Oliver asked hopefully.

"Like a charm," Mr Stewart assured him. "Sometimes with women it's not what you say, it's just having the guts to say something. Just be yourself, partner."

Just then, an ice-cream truck pulled up. Its jingly song, grating to everyone else, was music to Mr Stewart's ears.

"Now, if you'll excuse me, I think I've jogged my way to a Fudgybuddy," he told Oliver.

He tore off in hot pursuit of chocolate, leaving Oliver to mull over his advice.

Meanwhile, Jackson had his own personal struggles to deal with: Rico had arrived.

"Hello, Jackson," said Rico, sounding devilish.

"Hello, Rico."

"I want chicken wings," Rico said, knowing full well that his family's restaurant didn't offer chicken wings.

"We don't have chicken wings," said Jackson, wondering where Rico was going with this.

"Well, we should."

"Well, we don't."

What was Rico's deal? Jackson was tired from a full day of school and work, and wasn't in the mood to go head-to-head with him. "Come on, Rico, why do you always have to be so mean?" he asked.

"If I'm not telling my therapist at 200 bucks an hour, why would I tell you?" Rico retorted. "Now, back to chicken wings. Whose name is on that sign?"

"Yours."

Cooper started keeping score. "One for him," he said, gesturing to Rico.

"And whose father owns this place?"

"Yours," said Jackson with a sigh.

"That's two," Cooper counted.

"And whose father told you to keep Rico happy? Does this look happy?" Rico made a clownlike frown.

"Three in a row – tic-tac-toe!" shouted Cooper.

Jackson couldn't take it any more. "What kind of wings do you want? Mild, medium or spicy?"

When Rico let out an exultant "Spicy!" Jackson trudged off to the kitchen, wishing he were the one giving orders for once.

The next day at school, Miley and Lilly examined their work. Something wasn't quite right. What was it? The shirt? No, the shirt was cool. The trainers? No, those worked. The hair? Yeah, that was it. Miley surveyed the mess and decided what she needed to do. She placed her hands on Oliver's head and rubbed as if she were stroking a large, furry sheepdog.

"Just one more tweak and it's Becca time," she told him. "There. Just messy enough to say, 'I'm wild, but I can be tamed'."

A breath check was the next order of business. Lilly asked Oliver to open wide, took a whiff, then sprayed breath freshener into his mouth. At least, she'd meant to spray breath freshener . . . Oliver coughed, then looked like he might puke. He gaped accusingly at Lilly.

"That's perfume!" he cried.

Lilly glanced down at the bottle, apologized, then took another whiff.

"But it worked," she said with a shrug. "Are you ready?"

"I'm ready!" he shouted as if he were a football player and Lilly and Miley his coaches.

"Do you feel it?" asked Miley.

"I feel it!" answered Oliver.

"Are you da man?!" asked Lilly.

"I DA MAN!" yelled Oliver.

It was time. "Go, go, go!" shouted Miley.

When Oliver headed for the cafeteria, Miley and Lilly followed several steps behind.

✻ ✻ ✻

Oliver was pumped up. He was confident. His hair looked good. His breath smelled like a flower shop. And, hey, if Mr Stewart had got a date with 'My Robby name is hi', then Oliver could do just as well as that.

No, he could do better . . .

He puffed out his chest, took a deep breath and went for it.

Becca smiled the second she saw him.

"Hi, Oliver," she said cheerily.

This was it, the moment of reckoning. Oliver was psyched, he was ready. He looked into Becca's pretty, beaming face and said, "My Robby name is hi."

Ooof!

He thought about making a run for it. Ditching. Pretending that this had never happened. But then he saw Lilly and Miley out of the corner of his eye. What would they think

if he went down like that? Nope! Wasn't gonna happen. He had to rally. Becca was the one who liked *him*, after all! Oliver held up a finger as if to say hold on, then tried again. This time it went a little better.

"My Oliver name is hi," he said.

Not perfect, but Becca seemed to get the drift.

"Are you trying to ask me out?" she asked with a gentle smile.

"Yes. Wow. For a second there, I thought I was a babbling idiot." He turned to Lilly and Miley, who were lurking by the cafeteria queue, and gave them the thumbs-up. They cheered.

Miley looked at the cute couple, thinking nothing was more satisfying than matchmaking, especially when a good friend was involved . . .

Chapter Four

It was one thing for Rico to make Jackson cook chicken wings. It was *another* thing for Rico to make him wear a chicken suit and sing a song. A really lame song.

This was definitely Cooper's fault. It all went back to yesterday: it was the afternoon, they were hanging out, and Rico was bragging about how much his dad loved his chicken-wing idea.

"Wanna hear my next idea?" he asked.

"Oh, man, it doesn't involve him in a chicken suit, does it?" Cooper had joked, pointing a finger at Jackson.

"It does now!" Rico had evilly replied.

And now, a day later, here Jackson was, sweating in a hot feather suit, singing, "*Everybody dance, everybody sing, everybody try a free chicken wing*!"

Considering how silly he looked and how stupid the song was, you'd think people would ignore him. But they kept coming! And coming! Until a crowd surrounded him.

"Hey! Take it easy! Back off!" Jackson screamed. Soon he'd landed on his backside, cradling an empty bucket of chicken wings in his . . . chicken wings.

Through the flurry of loose feathers wafting in the air, he saw Rico standing above him with a camera phone in his hand.

"Tsk, tsk, tsk. Lying down on the job. Dad's not gonna be happy about this." And then Rico pointed his camera phone at Jackson's prone body and snapped a picture.

How much humiliation could one chicken take?

Chapter Five

The only reason Oliver had scored a date with Becca Weller was because of Hannah Montana. And without Miley, there would be no Hannah Montana. So by the transitive property of whatever it was her algebra teacher called it, Miley figured it was Oliver's obligation to tell her and Lilly every little detail of his date.

She and Lilly found him in his usual spot by the lockers. They didn't waste any time before they started the grilling.

"Oliver! What happened with you and Becca at the mall yesterday?" Miley asked him.

Lilly joined in. "Yeah, come on! Flap those lips!"

Oliver smirked. "Sorry, I don't kiss and tell," he said.

Miley couldn't believe her ears. "You kissed?"

"Tell!" ordered Lilly.

"My lips are sealed," insisted Oliver, who proved his point by opening his locker and sticking his head inside it. But then, because he couldn't hold back, he blurted out, "She thinks I'm funny, smart and sensitive! It was the greatest day of my life!" He pulled his head back out and then made a zipping motion over his lips as if to say that was it. "Zipped tight," he reminded them. He started to walk off, then stopped himself, turned back to his friends and whispered a sweet "Thank you!"

Miley could barely contain herself.

"This is wicked awesome!" she exclaimed, once Oliver was out of earshot. "Once again, Hannah Montana makes the world a better place for luuuv . . ."

"Becca must be so jazzed," Lilly commented. "I wonder if she's thanked Hannah yet. Check your email."

Miley blushed. "Oh, I don't do this for the thanks," she said. Then she removed her PDA from her pocket. She was curious to hear Becca's side of things, too.

"Come on, girl, spill your electronic guts," she said as she logged into Hannah's email account. Yup, she had some new mail. "Ooh. There she is," Miley said. She read Becca's latest email out loud. "'Dear Hannah, thanks for the great advice . . .'"

Lilly continued reading over Miley's shoulder. "'. . . too bad I have to end things with this guy who really likes me'."

The girls exchanged a look that said, *Uh-oh*.

Miley read: "'He's super-nice, but I have to tell him I just want to be friends'." Well, this was *not* what she'd been expecting. "She's going to dump Oliver!" Miley exclaimed.

Lilly couldn't believe it, either. "After only one day?"

"Yeah," said Miley, feeling a mix of shock and sadness, not to mention embarrassment for Oliver. How awful to be dumped after one day! And she couldn't help but feel a little guilty. This wouldn't have happened if it weren't for her, after all! Ever the optimist, she tried desperately to find the good in all of this.

"But look on the bright side," she told Lilly. "It is the longest relationship he's ever had."

It was the best she could come up with.

Chapter Six

Miley's mind was completely and totally blown.

"I just don't understand this," she said to Lilly. "Becca was so into Oliver. He thought things went great – why would she want to break up with him?"

As soon as the doors swung open to the cafeteria, Miley's question was answered. There, at a table in the corner, was Becca having a deep confab with another guy.

Miley couldn't help noticing that he was a really cute guy. And that the two were holding hands . . .

"That little tramp," she growled.

Before Miley and Lilly could even contemplate what to do next, Oliver breezed into the cafeteria. He looked so happy, so content, Miley couldn't let him see what they'd just seen.

As always, she and Lilly were thinking the same thing. Because as soon as they saw him, they each grabbed an elbow and turned him around.

"You don't want to go in there," Lilly warned him.

Miley didn't like lying, but she'd do it if she had to.

"Big food explosion," she told Oliver as they walked him out of the cafeteria. "Horrible. Tuna everywhere."

But Oliver looked sceptical. "What are you doing?" he asked.

Well, thought Miley, might as well get it over with. She got straight to the point. "You need to dump Becca," she said.

"What?" Oliver looked stunned.

"Trust us," Lilly said. "She's bad news."

"Real bad news," Miley agreed. "Like walkin' barefoot through a field of cows after their morning sit-down."

Miley had only recently moved to Malibu from Tennessee, which meant that sometimes Lilly and Oliver had no idea what she was talking about. They were used to some of her funny turns of phrase, but this one was a real doozy. They stared at her with unblinking eyes.

"What? Y'all never heard that one before?" Miley asked. She quickly got back to the point. "Oliver," she said, "Becca emailed Hannah. She said she just wants to be friends with you. I'm sorry."

Oliver's eyes popped – he looked as if he didn't believe it.

"It's true," Lilly confessed. "She's already got someone else."

They walked Oliver into the cafeteria so he could see for himself. Becca was still there, holding hands with the boy in question.

Oliver's face fell. "I don't understand. We're supposed to go to the beach this afternoon." Then it hit him. "Oh, no. She's going to dump me at the beach."

Miley didn't know what to say.

"You don't know that!" she protested.

What could she say to make Oliver feel better?

"I mean, she could dump you on the bus,

in the mall, in between classes – she could even text-message you."

Okay, not that.

"Why did you tell me she liked me in the first place?" Oliver asked, his shock turning into anger – with them! "This is all your fault," he said accusingly. "You and Hannah's stupid email advice! Why don't you stick to singing and your little dance moves!"

And then, after doing a mocking send-up of one of Hannah Montana's signature grooves, Oliver was gone.

Ouch, thought Miley. That hurt.

Chapter Seven

Miley was in a bad mood. And the last thing she wanted to hear when she was in a bad mood was a happy song. Especially one that she was supposed to sing.

When she got home from school, her dad greeted her at the door with a guitar in hand.

"Hey, Mile, I'm working on a new melody for Hannah," he said excitedly. "Sit down and tell me what you think."

It was the happiest, most chirpy song Miley had ever heard. And the only way she could think to respond was to pick up a throw pillow, shove her face into it and scream.

She screamed for a while. It felt surprisingly good, actually.

Once she'd calmed down enough to talk, she explained to her dad that it wasn't the song she hated. Then, she told him what had happened.

"I used Hannah's advice column to help Oliver get a girl," she said, "and ended up making things worse."

Sometimes Mr Stewart could be very blunt. "Then I guess it's all your fault," was his reply.

Sometimes Miley wondered what was going on in her dad's head.

"Whoa, you're not supposed to say that,"

Miley complained. "You're supposed to say I did it with good intentions and shouldn't be so hard on myself."

Her dad complied. "Okay, you shouldn't be so hard on yourself."

What was wrong with him? "How can you say that?" Miley cried. "I meddled, and now Oliver's miserable. You can't just let me off the hook for that."

"Okay, you're grounded," her dad said. He didn't sound very punishing.

"No!" Miley's voice was tinged with frustration. "This is where you hug me and say, 'Everything's gonna be all right, bud'." Did she have to tell him everything?

Poor Mr Stewart. There was nothing he could say that would appease his daughter.

"Mile," he said in his most soothing tone, "you tried something. It didn't work out." He looked into his daughter's despondent face. "Everything's gonna be all right, bud."

Miley hugged her father and heaved a sad sigh. As she watched him go, she made a decision: she was never meddling again.

Within seconds of Mr Stewart's departure, Lilly arrived at the Stewarts' house. She was holding on to a rope.

"Hey," said Lilly.

"Have you seen Oliver?" asked Miley.

Apparently the answer was yes, because when Lilly tugged on the rope, Oliver rolled in. He was on a skateboard.

"I hate my life, I hate my life, I hate my life . . ." he repeated.

Hearing her friend sound so sad made Miley's heart plummet. Lilly was less sympathetic. Maybe because she'd been hearing this for the last half hour.

"Enough, already!" she commanded. "How many times do I have to tell you? Dump her before she dumps you."

Miley sighed guiltily. After all, she was the reason he felt this way. She summoned up her energy and tried to sound as encouraging as possible.

"Lilly's right. I mean, you tried something that didn't work out." She needed to say something to help Oliver, to boost his ego. She took a deep breath. "You're Smokin' Oken!" she said in her most pep-squad way. "If she doesn't appreciate you, there are other girls out there who will."

Something seemed to have worked. Because when Miley finished, Oliver looked positively invigorated.

"You're right!" he shouted. "I'm gonna dump her!" With that, he rolled off.

Phew. Telling Oliver the truth had been

rough for Miley, but she was relieved she'd done it. She wasn't even in a bad mood any more. A good thing, because if she had been, she wouldn't have been able to appreciate the sight of her older brother Jackson padding downstairs on feathered feet. On . . . what? Jackson was wearing . . . a chicken suit! He had the headpiece perched on his forehead as if it were a visor.

"Nice being a pop star, isn't it?" he said sarcastically. "Guess what I don't want for dinner?"

Hamburgers? the devilish part of Miley wanted to say. But before she got a chance, Jackson slammed the door behind him. She turned back to Lilly, who was tap-tap-tapping away on Miley's PDA.

"What are you doing?" she asked.

"I'm going to give that Becca a piece of Hannah Montana's mind," Lilly answered.

"You are not. Hannah Montana's caused enough trouble."

Lilly ignored Miley. She'd already logged into Hannah Montana's email account. "Oh, look," Lilly said. "Becca wrote you again. How convenient."

Miley swiped the PDA away. She needed to see that traitorous Becca's email for herself. She read out loud, "'Dear Hannah, you were right. Oliver is such a great guy for me'."

Uh-oh.

"'So today in the cafeteria I broke up with my old boyfriend, Toby . . .'"

It took several seconds for the realization to hit.

"That's the guy she was holding hands with!" cried Lilly, who was already looking horrified.

"'Toby took it pretty hard. But now

Oliver and I can be together'."

Miley and Lilly gaped.

"Not if he breaks up with her!" Lilly exclaimed, sounding hysterical. "We have to stop him!"

"What are we standing here for?" Miley shouted. "Let's go!"

So much for never meddling again . . .

Chapter Eight

It was one thing for Rico to make Jackson cook chicken wings. It was another thing for him to make Jackson wear a chicken suit. It was a whole other thing for Rico to ask Jackson to wear a chicken suit while hanging from a parasail and flying across a beach – a beach that was full of beachgoers, all of whom would be watching as Jackson made a complete fool of himself!

Jackson had to take a stand. He told Rico he wasn't doing it.

"Oh, yes, you are," Rico said with a haughty laugh. "It's advertising, and my dad already paid for it."

"I don't care," argued Jackson. "I refuse to look ridiculous."

"Said the man in the chicken suit," replied Rico.

At that moment, Miley and Lilly came tearing across the beach.

"Have you seen Oliver?" Miley asked breathlessly.

"He's down the beach with some girl," Jackson told her, pointing towards a faraway spot across the beach. Just the mention of Oliver on a date made Jackson's current predicament seem even worse. He felt the anger rise inside him: he could feel his neck and face redden inside the mask.

"Because he can get a girl!" he added. "Because he's not in a chicken suit!"

Miley and Lilly didn't have time for Jackson's issues. They had their own to worry about. Oliver was far down the beach, too far for them to get to him before he did the deed and broke up with Becca.

"We'll never get to him in time," said Lilly woefully.

But Miley wasn't giving up. She'd got Oliver into this mess, she was getting him out of it.

"We have to!" she cried determinedly. "If I don't stop him, I'll never forgive myself."

"But how?" Lilly pointed to the specks in the distance that were Oliver and Becca. "Look how far away he is. You'd have to be able to fly!"

To fly! What to do? Miley racked her brain for answers.

She could play the Hannah Montana card, call her record company, see if they'd send her a helicopter. No, not enough time for that.

Maybe she could ask them to send her a boat instead, then she could borrow some water skis . . . no, that would take too long, too. Plus, she didn't know how to water ski.

Miley's mind was racing. Suddenly, it dawned on her: the answer was right in front of her. She turned to Rico. "Is that a parasail?"

Rico was no dummy. He immediately saw where Miley was going with this.

"Slow down there," he said. "There's only one way you get to go up in this thing . . ."

"You are one evil little boy," said Miley, shaking her head.

"It's a little too late for flattery," Rico replied with a mischievous grin.

All eyes were on Miley. She looked from Rico to Lilly to Jackson in that ridiculous chicken getup. She knew what she had to do.

It was all up to her.

Chapter Nine

Had it not been for the stupid costume Rico had forced her to wear, Miley would have been able to feel the warm Malibu wind brushing against her face and whipping through her hair. Instead, all she could feel was her right cheek rattling against the inside of the chicken head. Since it was meant to fit Jackson, the costume was too large for Miley. So seeing through the eye holes was very difficult. If she craned her neck in a certain way, she could catch a glimpse of Oliver and Becca, though they were still not much bigger than specks. She hoped she'd make it in time!

She wafted through the air, her feathers blowing in the breeze. She wondered whether seeing a giant chicken in the air would really help sell wings. It also struck her that chickens didn't know how to fly. She must be quite a sight for fellow birds.

Finally, Oliver and Becca came into view. She could see them, their heads bent towards each other in deep conversation. She hoped Oliver hadn't done it yet.

"Oliver!" she screamed. He didn't hear her. "Oliver!" No response. She was too high. "I need to be lower!" she told the guy piloting the boat.

He wasn't the smoothest sailor, and soon Miley was plunging through the air. But she still wasn't low enough. "Lower!" she yelled.

Her stomach lurched as she dropped another few feet. Then another. Until . . . *splash*! She hit the water.

"Thanks," she said, then sank.

As if the chicken suit wasn't already heavy! Miley was practically panting as she swam towards land. She didn't have to feel guilty about missing her appointment with Hannah Montana's trainer today: doing the doggy paddle while wearing a zillion-pound chicken suit was a serious workout.

She heaved herself onto the sand. She shook the seaweed from her wings. There before her were Oliver and Becca. She didn't miss a moment before hurling her body towards them, screaming, "Oliver! Wait! Don't do it! Don't say anything!"

It's not every day that a soggy human-size chicken emerges from the sea, then comes charging at you, screaming your name. Oliver looked shocked. He took several moments before putting two and two together.

"Miley?" he said in confusion.

Miley pulled the chicken mask off. "Please tell me I'm not too late."

"Miley," Becca asked, "why are you dressed like a chicken?"

"Because they were out of gorilla outfits," answered Miley a little sharply. She didn't have time for small talk. "Can we move on now? Oliver and I need a little time to talk . . . you know, face to beak."

She yanked Oliver by the collar and pulled him away while Becca looked on in dismay.

"You didn't break up with her, did you?" Miley asked in what she'd meant to be a hushed voice. Unfortunately, it was anything but, because Becca overheard.

"Uh . . ." Oliver hesitated.

"What?" Becca sounded angry. "You were going to break up with me?"

Oliver turned from Miley to confront Becca. "Well, you were going to break up with me," he said.

Apparently this information was news to Becca. "No, I wasn't," she argued. "Why would you think that?"

Oh, no! How had Miley messed up again? She didn't have time to come up with an explanation. Instead, she blurted out, "Because that's what you wrote Hannah Montana!"

Of course, this was a gigantic whopper of a mistake. Was she *trying* to give her identity away? Miley froze, not knowing what to do next.

"How did you know that?" Becca demanded.

"How did I know that?" a desperate Miley repeated, trying to buy some time. She was prepared to lie, but she couldn't even think of a good lie. She looked to Oliver for help. "How did I know that?"

"Because . . . you . . . read . . . minds." He looked from Miley to Becca. "There it is," he said.

Wow, Miley had hoped Oliver would have done better than that. "Well," she said, staring at him, "I'm reading yours right now, and I'm drawing a blank."

She'd have to do this herself. She turned to Becca. "Seriously, I didn't read your mind, that's ridiculous. I read . . . your PDA, which I stole from your gym locker."

As soon as the words left her mouth, she realized they weren't much of an improvement. Now Becca thought Miley was a petty criminal!

"Why would you do that?" Becca demanded.

"Because . . . I'm a baaaad chicken," said Miley. It was all she could think to say. Plus, it was kind of funny. And this situation was nothing if not a little funny.

Oliver jumped in to rescue Miley. "And, because she's in love with me!" he cried.

"What?" Miley sputtered.

"Yes. You don't have to hide it any more. Face it, you were nearly driven mad by the thought of me in the arms of another woman!"

Clearly, Oliver was having some fun himself. Miley had no choice but to go with it. "Okaaaaaay," she conceded. "What he said. But with less feeling."

Oliver couldn't help himself. He laid it on. Thick. "She's been in love with me for years," he told Becca. "A deep, needy–"

Miley interrupted him. "I think she gets it. The important thing here is nobody was breaking up with anybody. Oliver is a real special guy and you two are meant for each other."

Becca looked like she bought it. And soon, she and Oliver only had eyes for each other. Miley couldn't help but admire the happy couple with satisfaction. After all, if it weren't for her, they never would have got together . . .

Miley flapped her wings, let out a couple of clucks and said *adios*. It was time to head back to Rico's. She had so much to tell Lilly!

Part One

"This is so cool," said Lilly. "I can't believe how many people email Hannah Montana."

Miley read a particularly juicy email out loud. "Dear Hannah, I have this massive crush on a boy who doesn't know I exist'." It turned out that the email was from Becca Weller, a girl at Miley's school. And her crush was on Oliver!

The next day at school, Miley and Lilly watched Becca when Oliver came down the hall. "Did you see that?" Miley asked Lilly. "She totally checked him out."

"Couldn't you see that Becca Weller was hitting on you?" Miley asked.

Oliver took several moments to contemplate the news, then broke into a smile. "So, Becca Weller wants to take a ride on the Ollie Trolley."

"Sometimes with women it's not what you say, it's just having the guts to say something. Just be yourself, partner," counselled Mr Stewart.

The day after Oliver and Becca's date, Miley and Lilly couldn't wait to hear how the two had got along. "Oliver! What happened with you and Becca at the mall yesterday?"

After Miley and Lilly saw Becca holding hands with another boy, they broke the news to Oliver. "You need to dump Becca," said Miley.

Back at home, Miley and Lilly came up with a plan. "There's gotta be a way to stop him before he shops again."

But the plan didn't work. On Miley's birthday, she opened the present from her dad – only to find a dreadful kitty sweater! "I picked it out special for you, bud," he said.

When the kids at her birthday party made fun of the sweater, Miley took a stand. "I love this sweater, because it was given to me by someone I love very much."

Later that evening, Miley and her dad had a talk on the porch. "I guess a part of me wants to hold on to the little girl you used to be," Mr Stewart admitted.

PART TWO

Chapter One

Being a pop star was a big responsibility. Not only did you have to record really catchy songs, then perform them to sold-out stadiums full of screaming fans, you also had to become a household name.

A good way to do that was to make yourself the face for lots of cool and different products. Robby Stewart, father and manager to Miley Stewart, aka pop sensation Hannah Montana, could imagine a world of Hannah Montana merchandise. Think Hannah Montana surfboards. Hannah Montana mobile phones. Lip balm, flip-flops, moisturizer! Hannah Montana dog bones! Hannah Montana baby nappies! Okay, maybe sometimes he got a little carried away . . .

Scarves were the newest Hannah Montana items to hit the market. They were designed by the trendy French clothing designer Simone, and Miley was celebrating their debut with a meet-and-greet at a mall near her home in Malibu, California. Miley was used to getting a lot of attention, but there were still moments when she couldn't believe this was her life. Here she was, standing next to a mannequin dressed to look like Hannah Montana while a trembling queue of excited fans waited to meet her. Miley had never seen the teen section of the department store this crowded – not even on the weekend before the first day of school.

Even Roxy, Hannah's fearless and maybe-just-a-little-overzealous bodyguard, seemed rattled. "Okay, don't worry," Roxy told the crowd, "everybody who buys a scarf is gonna get a picture! Unless you make Roxy unhappy. And you don't want to make Roxy unhappy."

Roxy waved the next person in the queue over. It was a girl, giddy to be in Hannah Montana's presence. "This is so cool!" the girl clamoured enthusiastically. "I've been waiting months for these scarves to come out! I'm never taking it off!"

Miley found that the best way to keep her ego in check was not to take anything too seriously. "Great!" she told the girl. "Just be sure to shower in cold water only and lie yourself flat to dry."

The photographer snapped a picture.

"Okay, next!" shouted Roxy, shooing one girl away so another could come forward. But as soon as this next girl stepped up, Roxy stopped her in her tracks. "Not so fast, short stuff," she warned. She instructed the girl to hold her arms out, as she waved a security wand over her body. When she reached the girl's face, the wand let out an ear-piercing screech.

"I knew it!" Roxy sounded menacing. "What are you hiding in there?"

"Braces?" the girl answered meekly, then smiled nervously to reveal a mouth full of metal.

Apparently that wasn't evidence enough for Roxy. "Likely story," she snarled. "Open!"

When she shined a small torch into the girl's gaping mouth, Miley turned to Robby

Stewart and said, "Dad, Roxy's the best bodyguard we've had, but ever since she got back from her Marine Corps reunion, she's been a little in-your-face."

"She's just lookin' out for you, darling," her dad remarked. "Remember, Roxy's the same woman who threw herself between you and that sneezing fan in Cleveland."

Miley had to admit that was true. "You're right," she agreed.

Roxy completed her inspection. "She's clean. Doesn't floss, but she's clean. Move along." Miley smiled sympathetically as Roxy pushed the beleaguered girl forward.

While Miley signed autograph after autograph, smiling until her cheeks ached, her best friend, Lilly – dressed in disguise as Hannah Montana's right-hand gal, Lola Luftnagle – took the opportunity to browse.

But after banging heads with an obnoxious salesperson, Lilly had had enough. The salesperson's name was Milda, and apparently she didn't appreciate customers who looked and touched but did not buy. Lilly thought Milda was *r-u-d-e* rude, and made her way back to Miley.

"This is incredible," Miley said when she saw Lilly. "All these fans, and the store even made a mannequin of me!"

Lilly corrected her. "That's not a mannequin, that's a Hannahquin, Miss Montanaquin."

"Oh, no," said Miley with a groan.

"What?" Lilly had enjoyed her little wordplay! "That was cute-aquin," she contended.

But Miley's eyes were focused on something in the teen section, just past the Hannahquin. "I'm talking about my dad," Miley said, spying Mr Stewart as he browsed through the racks of clothes in the teen section. "I think he's looking for my birthday present."

"Oh, no," Lilly moaned, her voice dripping with sarcasm, "someone's gonna buy you something really expensive and cool. Whatever will you do?"

"You don't get it!" Miley cried as she watched her dad admire a hideous dress. "As a dad, he knows everything about everything. But as a shopper – the alarm should go off when he comes in the store."

They watched as Mr Stewart held the dress before him. He scratched his chin and nodded approvingly at it.

Lilly had to agree. "Wow. You ain't kiddin'. All that dress needs is a sheep and a bonnet, and you're Little Bo Geek." Lilly sniggered at her own joke – she was really on a roll today!

"I love him," said Miley, "but the man shouldn't be allowed in the teen department with a credit card."

She watched as her dad picked up another frilly monstrosity. She looked to the ceiling and moaned, "Will someone please stop him?"

What a mistake that was! Within seconds, Roxy came hurdling towards them. "Stop who? Where? I'll get him!" she shouted, tackling a shopper. Poor guy. He'd been looking for the men's shoe department and had got off the escalator on the wrong floor.

Miley and Lilly watched in horror as Roxy wrestled the man to the ground. It was several ugly seconds before they arose again. "He's clean!" Roxy announced.

Miley might have her father's bad taste to worry about, but at least she knew she was safe.

Chapter Two

Miley and Lilly were engaging in one of their all-time favourite activities: watching the clothing rack in Miley's wardrobe spin around and around. Miley's wardrobe was also Hannah Montana's wardrobe, which meant that in addition to Miley's modest school clothes, there were leather jackets by the dozen, jean jackets in every shade of denim, miniskirts, T-shirts and multiple pairs of cowboy boots.

Miley was still fixated on her dad's bad gift-giving habits. She didn't know why, but it really bugged her. "Mum always knew the right stuff to buy me. She had great taste. But Dad, man, he has the taste of a month-old pickle."

Lilly tried to imagine what a month-old pickle would taste like. She winced. "Look, no dad knows how to shop for a girl. Know what my dad got me for my last birthday? A savings bond – you can touch it, you can feel it, but you can't spend it! Pointless!"

Clearly, Lilly didn't understand the direness of the situation. Miley would be psyched to get a savings bond. Especially when she considered the gifts she'd received in the past. It was time, she decided, for her best friend to know the gory, gruesome truth.

The first awful gift Miley could remember getting from her father was a blouse, if you could call it that. To Miley, the blouse looked more like the doily her grandmother put out for Thanksgiving.

That was also the first gift she'd – there was no delicate way to put it – destroyed. Miley remembered the moment well: standing in front of the refrigerator, holding a glass of tomato juice in her hand, listening as her dad called for her. "Miley! Let's see that pretty new birthday number." She'd peeked around the corner to make sure he wasn't looking, then doused herself with tomato juice.

"Daddy," she'd asked in her most innocent-sounding voice, "does tomato juice stain?"

Then, there was the puffy-sleeved dress that had somehow crashed into the jug of grape juice; the fringed jacket that had met its unfortunate demise in a bizarre accident involving her dad's paper shredder. Last year's birthday, she'd gone the classic route: dumping an entire bowl of spaghetti and meatballs down her chest.

"*Mamma mia*!" exclaimed Lilly.

"This year," said Miley, "I'm thinking of mixin' it up a little – maybe a nice razzle-berry. It stains beautifully."

"Why don't you just say something to him?" Lilly asked.

"Because I don't want to hurt his feelings. You should see the look on his face when he gives them to me and says, 'I picked it out special, bud'." Miley imitated her father's droopy-eyed expression.

Lilly knew that one. "Ooh, the puppy-dog look," she said with a nod. "My dad got me to do summer school with that one."

"Well, I can't face that look again, and I can't face another one of these presents.

There's gotta be a way to stop him before he shops again."

"Well, what are you gonna do?" asked Lilly. "It's not like he's gonna take you with him."

Just then, an idea struck Miley. "True," she said, "but he might take you . . ."

Chapter Three

Jackson Stewart entered his house. He looked to the right. He looked to the left. "Miley?" he called. "Mile?" No response. Jackson breathed a sigh of relief. "Okay, the coast is clear," he said. "Bring in the cake."

He'd been talking to his buddy Cooper, who arrived seconds later carrying a large pink cake box. Cooper had a fondness for pranks, and as he entered the Stewarts' house, he pretended to trip over his feet and fall. "Whoa!" he yelled in mock alarm. He did it again. "Whoops!"

Jackson wasn't in the mood for Cooper's jokes. "Give me that!" He grabbed for the cake.

Cooper handed the box to Jackson. "Dude, chill, I'm playing with you. It's just a cake."

Jackson put the cake down on the worktop. Phew, it was safe. "It's not just a cake, it's Miley's birthday cake. And it's me proving to my dad that I can do something around here without screwing it up."

Cooper was well aware of Jackson's rep. "Dude, I can help you bring in a cake, but I can't help you with Mission: Impossible."

Jackson looked offended. "Hey, I got it here, didn't I?" He opened the pink box and peered inside. The cake was still there. Carefully, he removed it from the box. "Good, still perfect. And it's gonna stay perfect until Miley's birthday tomorrow. I just have to get it into the garage fridge. Grab the box. I can't wait to see the look on Dad's face when he gets a load of this cake."

Just Jackson's luck. It was at the very moment that he opened the kitchen door from the inside that his dad came charging in from the outside. Robby Stewart was carrying two six-packs of pop, which crashed to the floor just as the cake went flying from Jackson's hands. It was as if suddenly the cake had a mind of its own, because it made a beeline for Mr Stewart's head.

"Son," Mr Stewart intoned, a bit of icing hanging from his right ear, "I don't think you want to see the look on my face."

* * *

The next day, Miley and Lilly followed Mr Stewart to the mall. They trailed him, staying a safe ten steps away, as he re-entered the teen section of the department store. The Hannah Montana scarf display was still up, and the Hannahquin was still there.

"There he is," whispered Miley. "Just remember, my future happiness depends on you." She flashed Lilly a serious look. "No pressure."

Lilly was already nervous. "You know when people say 'no pressure'," she scolded Miley, "it adds more pressure."

Miley didn't have time for a discussion. She saw her dad fingering the most hideous sweatshirt known to teens. It was tie-dyed and emblazoned with rhinestones that formed the shape of a giant . . .

bunny?! Was that really a bunny? This was worse than Miley could have imagined. She looked at Lilly and exclaimed, "Just go!"

Lilly crossed the store to meet Mr Stewart, while Miley hid behind a sweater display.

"Mr Stewart! What on Earth are you doing here?"

Miley cringed at how unnatural Lilly sounded. Thankfully, Mr Stewart didn't notice. "Hey, Lilly, I'm still huntin' for just the right birthday present for my little girl."

"Well, what a coinkydink," said Lilly. "So am I. So, found anything?"

"Nope."

"Well, here's a wacky thought – maybe I can help you out, since I happen to be coinkydinkally here . . . coinkydinkally." Why couldn't Lilly stop using the word 'coinkydink'?

"Not a bad idea," replied Mr Stewart. He pulled a dress off the rack. "What do you think of this little number?"

It wasn't Lilly's opinion that mattered, it was Miley's. Lilly looked towards the display where Miley was hiding, hoping for a sign. She tried to stall. "Hmmm . . . what do I think of it? What do I think?" Her voice got louder with every word. From her hiding place, Miley signed 'No!'

"I'm gonna have to give that a thumbs-down," Lilly told Mr Stewart. "What about something over here?"

Miley watched as Lilly directed her dad towards another part of the teen section. Miley dashed behind a sales rack, scrambling to keep up. She peeked her head out of the rack of clothes and found herself face to face with Milda, the cranky salesperson.

"Hi," Miley chirped. "Just looking."

"Just wanted to let you know about our new promotion," Milda said sweetly. "It's called . . ." Milda's voice dipped. Now she sounded severe. ". . . buy something or get out!"

Milda dragged Miley from the rack and pushed her towards the exit. Now Miley was totally exposed. She tried to shield herself behind Milda.

"But, honestly," she spluttered. "I have my eye on some–"

Milda finished Miley's sentence for her. "–blah-blah-blah, bye-bye."

And Miley found herself kicked out of the teen section.

Chapter Four

Mr Stewart was getting frustrated.

"I don't know," he said, shaking his head. "Maybe we should try another store."

"No!" Lilly protested. She craned her neck looking for Miley. Where could that girl be hiding? "We haven't checked everywhere yet. I'm sure we can find her somewhere. I mean, find her something."

Miley listened to Lilly and her dad talk, and sniggered. She'd managed to sneak past Milda in the best disguise possible. As Hannah Montana . . . the mannequin, aka the Hannahquin.

It was a great disguise. It was also a risky one. Miley had to be speedy and stealthy. She gave Lilly a quick poke, then immediately froze in place.

"Lilly," she whispered through her frozen mouth.

"Whoa!" Lilly looked shocked as she put two and two together.

"What?" asked an oblivious Mr Stewart. "You find something?"

"Sure did," answered Lilly. Quickly trying to cover, she grabbed the first outfit she saw. Unfortunately, it was as hideous as anything Mr Stewart would have chosen. In fact, it might have been *more* hideous. "This," she said, handing the ugly garment to him.

Ack! thought Miley when she saw what her dad was inspecting. She knew what she was about to do was dangerous. If Milda saw the mannequin moving, not only would she kick Miley out again, she'd figure out that Miley was Hannah Montana. Still, she had to alert Lilly. She could not allow her dad to pay money for that hideousness! It was even worse than the notorious puke-green cardigan of 2003! In a flash of movement, Miley signalled 'NO!' to Lilly.

Thankfully, Lilly saw. "And I hate it," she told Miley's dad, snatching the outfit back. "Just thought you should know. Maybe there's something over here."

As Lilly led a befuddled Mr Stewart to another rack, Miley came across a jacket she liked. Or, rather, she came across a girl carrying a jacket she liked. It was such a cool jacket, Miley would have to take another risk. So when the girl walked past, Miley went to swipe the jacket. She tugged. The girl turned. Thinking the jacket had got caught on the mannequin's finger, the girl tried to pull it off. Miley held on tighter. The girl pulled harder.

"Let go," Miley hissed. She hadn't meant to sound so devilish and scary, but it was difficult *not* to sound that way when you didn't move your lips. And, anyway, it worked. The girl let go of the jacket and tore away in fear.

Promptly, Miley dropped the jacket on Lilly's head. Lilly managed to pull it off without Mr Stewart seeing. She presented it to him as if she'd just discovered a great item.

"Hey," he exclaimed, "that's nice! Where'd you find it?"

"It just kinda jumped out at me," Lilly explained.

"You think she'd like it?" he asked.

"I think if she were here," Lilly replied, "she'd be all over it."

"Well, then let's do it," said Mr Stewart. On their way to the tills, he glanced up at the mannequin. He looked a little awestruck. "Man, this thing is lifelike," he said. Lilly pushed him towards the tills, leaving a pleased Miley frozen in place.

Chapter Five

Why couldn't anything in his life be easy? On the morning of Miley's birthday, Jackson arrived home with a new cake. The only problem was, he couldn't get it inside the house. Jackson had lost his keys. He knew there was a spare set somewhere, but he couldn't find that, either.

As always, Cooper took the opportunity to rub it in. "First you drop a cake, then you lock yourself out of the house with the new cake. I'm starting to think you have a deep-seated resentment toward cake."

As always, Jackson did his best to ignore his friend. He put the cake down on the table and started to search. "Less thinky, more looky. If anything happens to this one, Dad'll never let me live it down . . ."

At which point, there was a giant thud.

It was rare to see a wild bird in Malibu, California. It was rarer yet to see a wild pelican. So Jackson was understandably shocked when he turned around to see one devouring Miley's cake.

"Whyyyyyyyyy?!" he yelled.

Cooper did his best to console his friend. "Maybe it's his birthday," he said.

Cooper's best . . . was not very good.

Miley's birthday festivities began after breakfast. Lilly had come over to hang out with the birthday girl and her family. So had Roxy.

Even though Roxy was there as a friend, she still had Miley's personal security at heart. So, when Lilly handed Miley a gift bag teeming with multicoloured tissue paper, Roxy got alarmed.

"Hold up there," she warned. "Has this bag been out of your sight or control at any time since you wrapped it?"

"Roxy, you're a guest. You're off the clock," Mr Stewart reminded her.

Roxy ignored him. "Mm-uhm. Danger never takes a vacation." She peered into the bag for several long seconds. "All clear . . ." she said finally. She snapped out of security mode when she turned to Miley and snipped, "And girl, you're gonna luuuvvv it!"

Miley removed an adorable purse from the gift bag. She grinned. "Lilly, this is awesome!" she cried, hugging her best friend. "It's gonna look so good with the jacket," she whispered.

"I know," Lilly whispered back.

Jackson was next. "Here you go, Mile," he said, handing her a box.

Roxy wouldn't have been Roxy if she hadn't interrupted to do another security check. "One second," she said, and reached for the box to check it.

Miley stopped her. "It's okay, Roxy. I'll get this one. And I'll use your present to do it." Roxy had given Miley a security wand. Miley waved it over Jackson's gift. "It's clean!" Miley announced triumphantly, as Roxy looked on proudly.

Miley opened Jackson's gift to find something . . . fuzzy?! *What was this*? It took Miley several seconds before it dawned on her. She gaped at her brother.

"Sheepskin seat covers," she drawled. Her brother was really something sometimes. "You gave me a present for your car?"

Jackson shrugged. "Hey, when I drive you to the mall, I want you to be comfortable." He smirked. "For Christmas, you're getting chrome spinners."

"Fine," replied Miley with a grin. "And you're getting a black leather skirt with matching pumps."

It was Mr Stewart's turn next. Lilly and Miley exchanged a mischievous look as a beaming Mr Stewart presented Miley with her gift. "Happy birthday, bud," he said sweetly.

Miley spent half her life acting, so it wasn't difficult for her to pretend to be psyched. Superpsyched!

"I have no idea what it is," she chirped,

"but that's the great thing about surprises, they surprise you." Miley opened the box, expecting to see the beautiful jacket.

Except . . . it wasn't the jacket.

It was . . . it was . . . Miley could barely wrap her mind around it! It was . . . a sweater with a giant picture of a kitten's face on the front. *Oh, no. What happened to the jacket*?

"And what a surprise this is," Miley spluttered.

Apparently hard-nosed Roxy had a soft spot. "Aw, it's a kitty," she cooed.

Looking as shocked as Miley, Lilly turned to Mr Stewart. In a hushed voice, she asked him what had happened to the jacket.

"Took it back. Didn't feel right," Mr Stewart whispered back to Lilly. He turned to Miley. "I picked it out special for you, bud," he said.

The sweater might have a cat on it, but Miley's dad was still working the puppy-dog eyes.

"I love it!" Miley lied to her dad. She turned the sweater over and tried to hide her dismay. "Especially the back," she said. On the back of the sweater was a giant . . . kitten . . . bottom.

"Do I know my little girl, or what?" Mr Stewart sounded thrilled with himself. "Squeeze the nose!"

Miley did as she was told. The sweater meowed.

"Just when I thought it couldn't get any cuter." Miley cringed, hoping she didn't look as aghast as she felt.

Chapter Six

Miley decided not to waste any time. What was that phrase? There's no time like the present? Well, today there was no time like the present . . . to destroy a present. Standing in front of the refrigerator, Miley told Lilly to keep a lookout.

She reached into the refrigerator. She'd done this so many times but still she felt a little nervous. The bottle was cold in her clammy hand. "All right, razzleberry," she said, "do your magic." She opened the bottle, then pulled the sweater away from her body – after all, she was wearing a cute T-shirt underneath! – and poured.

She peered down at the kitten in the centre of her sweater, expecting to see a giant razzleberry blotch. Except the kitten was clean and perfectly intact – it even seemed to be looking back at her and laughing!

"What the–" exclaimed Miley as she looked down to see a puddle of razzleberry on the floor. "Oh, man, this baby's stainguarded!"

Lilly was amazed. She took a closer look at the sweater. "I gotta know what's under the tail," she said curiously. She went to lift the tail, but Miley pulled away.

"Stop it!" she cried. "And nothing, I already looked." Miley couldn't believe her luck. She decided to give up for now, but not forever. "Okay, I'll wear it for an hour, make Dad happy," she said. "Then tonight, it will mysteriously fall into the barbecue."

Lilly spoke the unspeakable. "What if it doesn't burn?" she asked.

"I will cut it up and eat it if I have to," Miley answered. "Either way, no one besides me, you and my dad is ever gonna see me in this thing."

Just then, her dad called for her. "Hey, Mile, c'mon out to the deck. I got a little something else for ya."

She whispered to Lilly, "If it's the matching pants, you're eating with me."

"Surprise!"

It took Miley several moments to understand what was happening. Lilly was by her side. There were her dad and Jackson. There were Oliver and Roxy. And there was . . . her ENTIRE CLASS FROM SCHOOL! And she was wearing a kitten sweater!

Miley crossed her arms in an attempt to hide the atrocity, when she accidentally hit the nose. Miley might not have the words to describe how mortified she felt, but the kitten did.

"Meow."

"Gotcha, didn't I?" asked her dad.

"You sure did," a flustered Miley replied.

"Okay, everybody, down to the beach!" Mr Stewart called out to the party. "We've got a birthday to celebrate!"

As everyone headed for the shore, Miley hung back.

"Well, what are you waiting for?" her father wanted to know. "Get down there and show off that sweater."

Miley had to come up with something.

"You sure it wouldn't make the other kids jealous?" she asked her dad. "'cause it might. You know how kids are."

Her dad thought she was being silly. "Hey, this is your special day," he reminded her. "You deserve to have every eye down there on you."

Miley was out of ideas. "Great," she muttered and headed for the beach.

Everyone was having a good time. Everyone except Miley, that is. Mr Stewart had gone with a Caribbean theme: waiters served skewered jerk chicken and miniature spicy beef patties. There were giant frothy drinks – a mix of guava and pineapple juices served in glasses that looked like coconut shells. A band rocked out to Calypso music. Miley couldn't believe how awesome everything looked. If it weren't for her hideous attire, this would have been the most perfect birthday party ever.

There was even limbo. Usually, Miley aced any limbo contest, but there was *no way* Miley was going to do the limbo in a kitten sweater. Lilly tried to encourage her.

"Miley, c'mon," she said. "So it's a dorky sweater. No one here is gonna make fun of you. It's not like someone's gonna take a picture and put it in the school yearbook."

Miley still refused. Just then, Miley's classmates Amber and Ashley appeared.

"Hey, birthday girl!" they shouted. Miley and Lilly turned to see that each girl had a camera phone in her hand. "Say cheese!" they yelled.

"Cover my tail!" Miley cried, ducking behind Lilly. The two scurried off as Amber and Ashley snapped away.

Chapter Seven

Jackson stood over the kitchen worktop and stared at the mess. Who knew you could cause so much chaos in such a short time? All he'd been trying to do was bake a cake.

Jackson heard the door open and shut. "Yo, J-man! Jackson!" the voice called. It was Cooper.

"In the kitchen!" Jackson's voice was tinged with exasperation.

Despite the flour that was cascading off the worktop and the puddles of spilled milk on the floor, Cooper had no idea what Jackson was up to. "What are you doing?" he asked.

"What's it look like I'm doing?" Jackson shot back. He had no time for small talk. "I'm baking a cake." As he read through the recipe he started to pull all the ingredients into a bowl. "Okay, flour, milk. Now, add three eggs." He dropped the eggs, shell and all, into the bowl! "One, two and three."

"Uh, Jackson–"

Couldn't Cooper understand? He was busy! "Shh!" Jackson said, looking at the recipe once more. "Now, stir." He stirred. His spoon hit something hard. He put his hand in the bowl and pulled out . . . an unbroken egg. "I think there's something wrong," he moaned.

Cooper scowled. "You're supposed to break the eggs, fool!"

Oh! thought Jackson. He was feeling a little dumbfounded. How come he hadn't thought of that? Jackson held the egg in his hand and made a fist. His hand filled with messy yolk. He dumped it, along with the shattered shards of shell, into the bowl.

Cooper had had enough. "I can't watch this any more!" he cried.

Jackson stared disbelieving at his friend. "Like you could do better?"

Cooper got serious for a second. "Way better," he said. Jackson realized he'd never heard Cooper sound so solemn. Cooper lowered his voice. "Okay, I'm going to tell you something nobody outside my family knows," he whispered.

"You still drink Shirley Temples?"

"They're fruity and refreshing!" Cooper

answered. "But that's not it! The truth is . . ." Cooper took several seconds to finish his sentence. Finally, he blurted it out. ". . . I'm a baker."

"What?"

Cooper sounded relieved to have finally said it. Now he was ready to tell all. "I love to bake!" he cried. "Pies, cakes, tarts – and my snickerdoodles are off the chain!"

Jackson thought back to the snickerdoodles he'd sampled at Cooper's house. They had been mighty tasty. "You said your mum made those!"

"You kiddin'?" Cooper guffawed. "My mum can't make ice. Now move aside and let the pro have a go. I need a clean bowl, fresh ingredients and . . ." he snatched Jackson's apron off his body, ". . . gimme that. You're not fit to wear an apron!"

Jackson gladly handed Cooper the

apron. Phew, he thought. Boy, did he feel relieved. Then again, Cooper had better be as good as he claimed to be – Miley's party was halfway through and it was nearing time for the cake.

Chapter Eight

Miley couldn't believe it. Amber and Ashley just wouldn't give up. They'd discovered Miley's hiding place and were refusing to leave until she showed her face and posed for a photo. From behind the closed door, Miley heard Amber calling to her.

"Here, kitty, kitty, kitty," she taunted.

"Miley, you can't stay in the bathroom forever," Ashley yelled. For the first time in her life, Miley agreed with something Ashley said. She was sick of being in the bathroom. Plus, she was beginning to feel a little claustrophobic.

"Why don't you just take it off?" Lilly asked, pointing to the sweater.

"And tell my father what?" Miley wanted to know. She felt slightly dizzy, and it seemed like the walls were beginning to close in on her.

"I don't know," Lilly replied. "That you're allergic to cats?"

To show Lilly what she thought of that idea, Miley flushed the toilet.

"Well, you're gonna have to do something," Lilly told her. "If they take your picture, it'll be in the yearbook forever."

There was a knock at the door. Miley was ready to give Ashley and Amber a piece of her mind. But it was Oliver, fresh from his loss in the limbo contest, in which Roxy had pulled ahead at the last second.

"Miley, you can come out now," he said. "I got you covered."

Miley and Lilly exchanged a look. "How?" Miley wanted to know.

"Just trust me," said Oliver.

Miley opened the door a crack and got an eyeful of coloured plastic. What the . . . ?

"Here, this should cover the sweater," said Oliver, handing her a giant beach ball.

"Oliver, you're a lifesaver," said Miley happily. She opened the door and took the ball from him.

"My aunt Harriet got me the puppy version for Christmas," Oliver said. "It barks 'Jingle Bells'. I feel your pain."

Miley thought she was in the clear. But Ashley and Amber were more relentless than she could have ever imagined. They were not about to admit defeat.

"Very clever," mocked Amber.

"There's no way we can take that picture now," snipped Ashley.

"Right," added Amber with a wink. "Unless we were to do something like this."

Suddenly, Amber and Ashley resembled gunslingers from the old Western movies Miley's dad liked to watch. Except they didn't reach into their holsters for weapons, they reached into their hair. Before Miley knew what was happening, Amber and Ashley were using hair slides to stab at the beach ball. It deflated in Miley's arms.

"C'mon, stop it!" Miley cried.

Lilly and Oliver ran in front of her to try to protect her. "Why are you guys so mean?" Lilly asked.

"It's what we do," Ashley said smugly.

"Well, we don't," countered Lilly. "You

think everybody here doesn't know it's the dorkiest sweater in the history of the world?"

"You'd have to be blind not to see that!" added Oliver.

Miley was relishing the moment! Her friends sticking up for her like that! But then she saw that her dad had appeared behind them. Apparently, he'd heard every word that had just been said, because he looked hurt.

Miley looked from her friends to Ashley and Amber to her dad. To think she'd thought puppy-dog eyes were bad. Now her dad's entire face was drooping in despair! What had Miley done?

She stood there, holding the empty beach ball, feeling sick inside. Suddenly, it all seemed so silly. Missing a surprise party thrown in her honour because of a . . . cat sweater? Sneaking around a department store, pretending to be a mannequin, risking exposing her secret identity all because she didn't want her dad to buy her a bad gift? Miley couldn't believe herself. She had to make it better.

"Well . . . I don't care what anybody thinks," she declared. She let go of the sagging beach ball. "I . . . love this sweater," she said. "At least I do now. Because it was given to me by someone I love very much. So if you wanna take a picture, go ahead. Because this sweater means more to me than the coolest outfit in the world. Right, Mittens?" Miley pressed the cat's nose. The sweater really had a way with words.

"Meow," it said.

Amber looked remorseful. "Wow," she said to Ashley. "It really makes you think twice about taking the picture." Ashley nodded meekly.

But, just when it seemed like they might retreat, they reconsidered. "Say cheese!" they yelled at once. Miley squinted into the flash.

Great. Not only was she wearing a cat sweater, she also had her eyes closed.

Chapter Nine

Roxy to the rescue! Finally, the bodyguard's over-eager tactics paid off.

Just moments after Amber and Ashley snapped their last humiliating shot, Roxy appeared. She was holding on to her prize limbo stick, and it just so happened to find its way under Amber and Ashley's ankles.

Everyone knew that Amber and Ashley did everything together: they ate together,

shopped together and were mean together. Now, Miley watched as Amber and Ashley tripped together. They flew off their high-heeled flip-flops, screeching as they hurtled into the air. Miley hoped they'd crash into each other. Sadly, they didn't. Instead, they crashed into Cooper and Jackson, who just so happened to be carrying Miley's birthday cake.

"Noooooooooooo!" shrieked Jackson.

"Oh, yeah!" Roxy said, looking at Ashley and Amber, their heavily made-up faces smeared with icing. "That's what happens when you mess with Crouching Tiger, Hidden Roxy."

Cooper had spent most of the day laughing over spilled cake. Not this time.

"My cake!" he wailed. Hearing how incriminating that sounded – no one could ever know he was a baker! – he immediately tried to cover. "That I carried but didn't make . . . 'cause guys don't do that."

Meanwhile, Mr Stewart was taking matters into his own hands. He stood over Amber and Ashley, and removed his camera phone from his pocket.

"Ladies," he said, "say gotcha!" He snapped a photo. "Now we all have pictures," he said with a laugh. "Wanna trade?"

Miley beamed at her dad. She had never felt so proud.

That evening, when the party was over, Miley found her dad sitting by himself, looking out at the ocean.

"Dad," she said.

"Hey, sweetheart," he replied.

Miley sat down next to him. "Thanks for a great birthday party."

"And thank you for what you said out

there. But we both know I messed up, don't we?"

Miley's stomach sank. Her dad hadn't messed up. She had. She struggled for the right words to say. "It's not . . . I wouldn't . . . it meows, Dad."

"I know. Funny thing is, I looked at plenty of clothes I bet you would've liked a lot, but I just couldn't buy 'em."

Well, this was confusing. "Why?" Miley asked. "You see what I wear to school. You see me up onstage as Hannah Montana."

"Maybe that's why," said Mr Stewart. "It's just that you're growing up so fast, I guess a part of me wants to hold on to the little girl you used to be."

Miley's heart melted like the icing on her birthday cake in the Malibu sun. "Aw, Daddy. I'll always be your little girl," she said. "I just wanna be your little girl who dresses better."

"You know what? When your mum was around, she'd always shop for the presents and my job was to carry the bags. Maybe it's time I started carrying your bags."

Miley liked the sound of that. "That could work," she said.

"Just one thing, when you open your presents, could you still act surprised?"

Miley could do that. She even proved it by gasping in surprise.

"That's perfect," Mr Stewart said.

They sat staring at the water, thinking about everything that had happened that day, when the strangest thing happened. A pelican hopped by, and it might have just been Miley's imagination, but it sure looked as if that pelican had icing on its beak!

Put your hands together for the next Hannah Montana book . . .

Adapted by Laurie McElroy

Based on the television series *Hannah Montana*, created by Michael Poryes and Rich Correll and Barry O'Brien

Based on the episode written by Sally Lapiduss

Miley Stewart closed her eyes and fell back into Lilly Truscott's arms. She wasn't scared. Miley trusted Lilly. She knew her best friend would catch her, just like Miley had caught Lilly a few minutes before. That's what friends did for each other.

Mr Corelli, Seaview Middle School's

drama teacher, checked out the pairs around the classroom then jumped onto the stage. "Very nice, people," he said. "Now that you have clearly mastered the trust exercise, you're ready to act."

Miley's eyes lit up. Acting was the reason she had signed up for drama class in the first place.

"But," Mr Corelli said, "the secret to acting is . . . reacting." He jumped in front of Miley's other best friend, Oliver Oken, and screamed in his face.

"Aaaaa!" Oliver shrieked, falling back into his partner Henry's arms.

Mr Corelli seemed pleased. "Did you see that?" he asked the class. "He reacted. He didn't think. Did you?" he asked, turning to Oliver.

"I try not to, sir," Oliver stammered, saluting.

"And you're great at it," Mr Corelli said, saluting back.

Oliver was confused. It was the first time he'd ever been praised for not thinking.

"I want you all living in that moment," Mr Corelli said, slowly moving in front of Miley. Suddenly he spun around. "Aah!" he yelled, right into her face.

Miley didn't flinch. She didn't even blink. "I've got a brother," she explained. "You're going to have to do way better that."

"Oh," Mr Corelli said nodding. He turned away, and then spun around again. This time it was Lilly he screamed at.

Lilly jumped back and screamed, just like Oliver.

"Nice work," Mr Corelli said. "You get an A for the day."

Lilly wasn't impressed. Mr Corelli was

definitely the strangest teacher she had ever had. "I'll take a B if you stop doing that," she said.

The rest of the kids in class braced themselves. Who would Mr Corelli pounce on next? But instead, he jumped back onstage. "Everybody, listen up! Now we're going to do the mirror exercise. What one does–" he raised his right hand and wiggled his fingers, "–the other mirrors," he said, raising his left hand and wiggling his fingers the same way.

Miley watched him and nodded.

"Acting," Mr Corelli said, holding his right hand in front of him like the signal for stop. "Reacting," he explained, doing the same with his left hand. Then he moved his hands together. Whatever his right hand did, his left did too.

Miley looked at Lilly and rolled her eyes.

Mr Corelli was way too in love with his own hands.

He waved his finger in the air like a conductor's baton. "Mirror," he announced.

The pairs from the trust exercise stood face to face, mirroring each other while Mr Corelli walked around the room, checking them out. He stopped in front of Oliver and Henry.

"Now, next week," he said, "we're doing scenes from Shakespeare's great play *Romeo and Juliet.*" He struck a dramatic pose. "'But soft, what light through yonder window breaks? It is the East, and Juliet is the sun'," he said, quoting Romeo.

Oliver and Henry tried to mirror him – and each other – but Mr Corelli was too caught up in his own acting to notice.

"Man, that dude knew how to pick up

chicks," Mr Corelli said, pumping his fist in the air.

Lilly and Miley tried to have a quiet conversation while Mr Corelli made his way around the room.

"So, who do you want for a partner?" Lilly asked.

"Well, not Oliver," Miley answered, making a face. "I mean, look at him."

Lilly turned to see Oliver scratching himself and hooting like a chimpanzee. Henry was mirroring him.

Lilly snorted. "I know. He's always monkeying around." She scratched her head and her side like a monkey when she said it.

"Exactly!" Miley cried, mirroring her. "And I need a good grade."

"So do I," Lilly said. "But if one of us doesn't pick him, nobody will."